Mel & Mo's
Marvelous
Balancing Act

For Carole with love.
—NW

To my other half, who keeps
me balanced every day.
—MF

We acknowledge the support of the Canada Council for the Arts and the
Ontario Arts Council, and the participation of the Government of Canada/
la participation du gouvernement du Canada for our publishing activities.

Canada   ONTARIO ARTS COUNCIL
CONSEIL DES ARTS DE L'ONTARIO
an Ontario government agency
un organisme du gouvernement de l'Ontario

Library and Archives Canada Cataloguing in Publication

Title: Mel and Mo's marvelous balancing act / Nicola Winstanley ; [illustrated by] Marianne Ferrer.
Names: Winstanley, Nicola, author. | Ferrer, Marianne, 1990- illustrator.
Identifiers: Canadiana (print) 20190070021 | Canadiana (ebook) 20190070056 | ISBN 9781773213248
(hardcover) | ISBN 9781773213279 (PDF) | ISBN 9781773213255 (EPUB) | ISBN 9781773213262 (Kindle)
Classification: LCC PS8645.I57278 M45 2019 | DDC jC813/.6—dc23

Published in the U.S.A. by Annick Press (U.S.) Ltd.
Distributed in Canada by University of Toronto Press.
Distributed in the U.S.A. by Publishers Group West.

Printed in China

annickpress.com

Also available as an e-book. Please visit annickpress.com/ebooks for more details.

Mel & Mo's Marvelous Balancing Act

written by
Nicola Winstanley

illustrated by
Marianne Ferrer

annick press
toronto • berkeley

Mel and Mo were twins.

They loved one another
and looked just the same.

I like the
ice cream.

But they liked different things.

I like the rain.

Until they fought all the time because they could never agree.

I get up early!

When they grew up, Mel bought a tidy house and took over the family umbrella store.

I want to make things!

Mo ran away to the Sunny Seaside Circus.

I want to perform!

For many years, Mel made sturdy umbrellas
that never blew inside out or upside down.

And Mo circled the big top on a unicycle, a poodle
on each shoulder, to thunderous applause.

But tastes and fashions change . . .

And one day, Theodora Tweedle's Spectacular Raincoats and Roller Skates came to town.

After that, rainy-day roller skating in spectacular raincoats became all the rage.

No one wanted Mel's umbrellas anymore.

And no one cared to watch
Mo unicycle with poodles.

It was old hat.

Mel began to make bigger
and more beautiful umbrellas.

And Mo began to learn
a more exciting trick.

But although the rain fell every day,
Mel didn't sell a single umbrella.

Mo fell every day, too—off the high wire and into the big net below.

Mel and Mo both
needed something.

But neither of them
could think what it was.

After that, Mel made the world's best, super-duper, handmade umbrellas for all the performers in Mo and Theodora's brand-new Roller Skate Umbrella Circus.

Despite their differences, for the rest of their lives,
Mel and Mo lived happily together—in balance.